You and Me

and the wishing tree

Nancy Tillman

FEIWEL AND FRIENDS

NEW YORK

We woke up in the usual way,
but it was *not* a usual day.

Out on the lawn,
plain as could be,
stood an orange wishing tree.

"I wish!" said I.
"I wish!" said you.

And so, our double wishes grew.

I kept my wish a secret one,
but you were not so shy.
You clapped your hands,
jumped off the bed, and said,

"I WISH TO FLY!!!"

In just a whistle's worth of time
and not a second more,
our feet were not attached to ground
the way they'd been before.

Up we went, just you and me,
high above the wishing tree.

We flew in silence,
like the birds.

It was too beautiful for words.

But your wishing wasn't done.
Why should you just stop with one?

In the valley, far below,
down where all the wishes grow,
your wishes grew, both big and small,
till I could hardly count them all.

In fact, I barely got to ten
because you wished for breakfast then.

"I wish," you said,
and just like that,
the friends you wished for
came and sat.

"I wish! I wish! I wish!" you shouted.

Wishes bowed . . .

and played . . .

and sprouted.

Every wish was wishable . . .
even *you*, invisible.

But as the day began to end,
your wishes became quieter then.

I saw your silly sleepy head
was wishing it was back in bed.

And so, I did what parents do.
I picked you up and carried you.

As you drifted off to sleep, you whispered,
"Did your wish come true?"
I whispered back, "My little one,
my wish was just to be with you."

THE WISHING TREE

Listen for it in the breeze.
It's not like all the other trees.
With every rustle, puff, and swish,
it says, "I wish. I wish. I wish."

To Shay Daniel Carlucci and his great, big, beautiful heart.
—N.T.

A FEIWEL AND FRIENDS BOOK
An Imprint of Macmillan

Printed in the United States of America by Phoenix Color, Hagerstown, Maryland.
For information, address Feiwel and Friends, 175 Fifth Avenue, New York, N.Y. 10010.

Our books may be purchased in bulk for promotional, educational, or business use.
Please contact your local bookseller or the Macmillan Corporate and Premium Sales Department
at (800) 221-7945 ext. 5442 or by e-mail at MacmillanSpecialMarkets@macmillan.com.

Library of Congress Cataloging-in-Publication Data Available

ISBN: 978-1-250-05629-0

The artwork was created digitally using a variety of software painting programs on a Wacom tablet. Layers of illustrative elements are first individually created,
then merged to form a composite. At this point, texture and mixed media (primarily chalk, watercolor, and pencil) are applied to complete each illustration.

Feiwel and Friends logo designed by Filomena Tuosto

First Edition: 2016

2 4 6 8 10 9 7 5 3 1

mackids.com

You are loved.